The Hat Trick

by
Terry Deary

Illustrated by Martin Remphry

First published in 2000 in Great Britain by
Barrington Stoke Ltd
18 Walker St, Edinburgh, EH3 7LP

This edition first published 2012

www.barringtonstoke.co.uk

ISBN: 978-1-78112-129-0

Printed in China by Leo

Contents

Chapter 1
Magic Hat Trick

The great thing about football is the memories it gives you. I've seen matches that were so exciting I'll remember them for the rest of my life … even if I live to be a hundred and thirty-seven.

But there's one match I'll remember till I'm two hundred and thirty-seven. It's one I played in over 40 years ago. The Boxing Day game, where I scored three goals for the first and last time in my life.

Of course it was my dad that got me interested in the game. "I could have played for England, Jud!" he used to tell me as we kicked the ball from one end of our little back garden to the other.

"Why didn't you, Dad?"

"I was too busy winning the war," he said.

When I was really young, I used to believe dad was a gun-shooting hero! As I grew older, I found he was a cook at the army camp and I was a bit disappointed.

When I grew much older, I understood what he meant when he said, "We all played our part to help win the war. Even if what we did didn't seem important. Just as a goalkeeper at the back doesn't score goals but is as important as the men at the front who do all the shooting."

He thumped the ball and it flew past my ear and buried itself in the hedge. "Dad ten – Jud one!" he used to say and go inside for a cup of tea.

He usually beat me ten – one ... that's when he wasn't beating me ten – nil. But I didn't mind. He wasn't one of those dads who was soft and let his kid win. He was tough and he was fair and I learned more that way.

That Christmas Eve I think I managed to lose just ten – two!

And that was the Christmas I'll never forget. We had Christmas lunch, then we sat by the Christmas tree to open our presents. I tried to look pleased with the jumpers and gloves and the books and board games and chocolates ... but there was nothing really exciting. And no toys this time.

"You're getting a bit old for toys," Mum said, "so your dad has no excuse to buy any for himself."

Gran sat in the corner and chuckled. The year before, Dad had bought me a train set then spent the next two days playing with it!

"No, Mum," I sighed.

Dad clicked his fingers. "Here, Jud!" he cried. "I wonder if there's anything in the magic hat?"

"Ohhhh! The magic hat!" I whispered.

Gran smiled as she gazed into the coal fire. She knew what Dad was going to do next.

Dad had learned a few magic tricks to entertain the soldiers in the war. He used them to give me special surprises for my birthday. He did a magic act for my friends at my party and always ended by pulling a special present from his top hat. He'd never used it at Christmas though.

He took the hat from the cupboard and I was thrilled. I had no idea what would come out this time. I got so excited I never watched carefully enough to see how he did the trick. Whenever I asked him he would just shrug and say, "Why, it's magic, of course!"

"Say the magic words, Jud!" he commanded in a booming voice.

"Abracadabra, hocus-pocus!" I said.

Somehow he seemed to pull the package from an empty hat. He did! I'll swear he did!

Gran nodded happily but Mum pressed her lips tight. I didn't know what was in the package but I did know she didn't approve.

I ripped the paper off so fast I scared the cat. She ran into the kitchen and the dog got excited and chased after her. I held the present in my hands as if it were solid gold.

"Boots!" I said and my eyes filled with tears. "Football boots!" I repeated over and over again. I was sniffing back the tears. Dad was trying hard not to sniff too. Mum was trying hard not to smile. "Thanks, Dad," I said finally.

"And your mum," Dad said.

"Thanks, Mum."

"You're spoilt," she said.

Chapter 2
Rubbing Dubbin

Of course I wanted to put them on, run out and play right there and then. But Dad said, "Football boots are leather and they'll crack if you get them wet in this weather."

It was true. In those days, boots were plain brown leather with a heavy toecap that would crush a tortoise.

"What do I do, Dad?"

"You rub dubbin into them," he said wisely.

"I thought Dobbin was a horse," I said stupidly and Gran cackled.

"The word is dub-bin. It softens the leather and protects it. We'll do it now and they should be ready to wear tomorrow," he said.

"Have you got some?" I asked.

"Under the kitchen sink," he said. "It's what I used on my boots before the war."

We spent the next hour rubbing the stinking, greasy stuff over every inch and into every seam of those boots. We rubbed them till they were warm.

"That's the way to make sure the dubbin soaks in," Dad explained. We even rubbed

dubbin into the leather laces. The boots sat under the Christmas tree and shone.

"They look like a pair of Aladdin's lamps," I told Dad.

We'd seen the pantomime two days before Christmas. I'd decided that if I had Aladdin's lamp, I'd wish for a pair of football boots.

They were the best present I'd had. They were the best I'll ever have if I live to be three hundred and thirty-seven.

"Of course, they're magic," Dad said.

"Get off," I laughed. But Dad wasn't laughing and Gran sat in the corner and nodded wisely.

"These boots have a magical mind of their own," he said.

"They haven't!" I argued, but I wasn't so sure now.

"Paid extra for it, I did," Dad insisted. "You'll see."

"When? When can I try them, Dad?"

"Tomorrow morning in the local park, Jud. I'll take you down there and you can try them out."

That was it. That was the end of Christmas. All I wanted was for Boxing Day to arrive. Most kids can't get to sleep on Christmas Eve because they're so excited. But I had trouble sleeping that night before Boxing Day. I couldn't wait for the hands on my alarm clock to crawl round. I couldn't wait for the sky to lighten.

I couldn't wait for the excitement to start. Of course I didn't know just how great that excitement was going to be.

Chapter 3
Redby Rivals

I shook Dad awake at six o'clock the next morning. He told me to go away … but those weren't the words he used. He wasn't that polite.

At seven o'clock, I took him a cup of tea. He groaned, "These are the only two days I get off till Easter weekend. I'm back in the shop tomorrow."

"Yes, Dad. Can I try the boots on now, Dad?"

"You can. But don't go clattering over the kitchen floor in those studs or you'll have your mum clattering in your ear."

"No, Dad," I said and raced downstairs.

I loosened the laces and put the boots on over my short white socks. They fitted like Cinderella's magic slipper – that was the pantomime we'd seen the year before – and were as snug as the old tennis shoes I wore for gym.

I stood in the middle of the living room floor and practised shooting an imaginary football. The fireplace was the goal and I made all my own sound effects. Foof! As I blasted the shot. Wahhhh! As the crowd roared its praise. The dog hid behind the chair. (She was always a coward like that.

Dad reckoned she made a good guard dog because she would lick burglars to death.)

At nine o'clock, Dad finally came downstairs. He wore his overcoat and scarf.

It was grey and chilly out there, but I wore my white shorts and the green sweater that Aunt Doris had knitted for me for Christmas.

"Right, Jud! Come on over to the park and I'll show you how Stanley Matthews won the 1953 Cup Final for Blackpool."

There was a fine mist blowing in off the sea and the streets were deserted. Dad made me change into my shoes for the walk to the park.

"You'll wear the leather studs out on the concrete pavement," he warned me.

I tied the boot laces together and slung them over my shoulder proudly. It was only a ten minute walk to the sea front where the dull water looked as lifeless and colourless as the sky. Then five minutes along the sea front to the park. That's where we saw the first signs of life that morning. Two groups of boys were changing into football strips on one of the park's soccer pitches.

I knew the strips at once. The black-and-white stripes were from Redby Junior School, a mile away from our house and our deadliest rivals in everything. The team in the green-and-white quarters was Seaburn Junior School. Our school.

I forgot about my kick-about with Dad. This was a real match. I was too shy to practise alongside these players.

Dad looked at me. "What's wrong, Jud?"

"They're top class, Dad!" I said.

"How do you know?" he asked. "You haven't seen them play."

"No! I mean they're the top class – fourth years. The big lads in our school. I'm just a third year."

"So why are they playing on a Boxing Day? Where's their teacher? Who's the ref?"

"I don't know, Dad."

"Then let's ask them, shall we?"

I felt a blush begin to rise from the bottom of my new boots all the way to the top of my hair. My face was burning. But Dad pretended not to notice. "Hey, lads!"

A big boy with fair hair scowled across at Dad. I knew he was Larry Potts, the captain.

"What?" snapped Larry.

"Is this a proper match?" asked Dad.

"It's a local derby," Larry said and stuck his fists on his hips. "The match was a draw when we played in the league last month. This is the decider."

"Want a ref?"

Larry Potts looked across at the Redby captain.

"Better had," the dark-haired boy from Redby agreed.

"Then I'm your man," Dad said and trotted happily into the centre circle. He left me alone, lonely, shivering and embarrassed on the touchline.

I decided, there and then, I would never forgive my dad, not if I lived to be four hundred and thirty-seven.

But that was before the boots showed their magic, of course.

Chapter 4
Mud and Blood

There was an argument before the game even started. "You have to have a goalkeeper," Dad said to our captain.

Larry Potts glared at him. "Stevie Mann is our keeper. But his mum said he had to go to their auntie's house in Blackfell for Christmas night and he'll be late back."

"Then you'll have to put an outfield player in goal!" Dad insisted.

The Seaburn players turned away from their captain or looked at the ground and whistled. No one wanted the job.

Dad pointed across at me. "Then let our Jud go in goal for you," he said.

The team looked at me with scorn. "A little third year!" Jimmy Archer laughed.

Larry Potts glared at him. "You go in goal, then!" he said.

"Nah!" Jimmy spat. "Let the kid go in goal. Better than nothing."

"It's not allowed in the league rules," the Redby captain argued. His name was Alan Bourne.

A couple of years later, I ended up in the same secondary school as Alan and he was a smashing lad. But right now he looked as if

he was sneering all the time and he was the enemy captain. I hated him!

"But this isn't a league match," I shouted.

"Yeah!" Larry Potts agreed. "Are you scared of letting the kid go in goal in case you get beat?"

"No! I'm scared in case the kid gets hurt."

"Look," Dad butted in. "I'm Jud's dad. I'll take the blame if something goes wrong."

Alan Bourne looked unhappy but he sniffed and said, "Let's get on with it, then."

As it happened I had Aunt Doris's new, green Christmas jumper on so I was perfect for the job. Well, I may have been a bit on the short side. Even with my biggest jump I couldn't reach the junior-sized crossbar.

As Jimmy Archer so kindly put it, "Better than nothing, I suppose."

So I found myself playing in the team behind all my Saturday morning heroes. Charlie Carter (named after a famous footballer) was as skilled as a ballet dancer, Dave Small was a terrier in the tackle and, of course, Larry Potts was a rock in the centre of defence.

The field was muddy, the ball kept sticking and there were a lot of sliding tackles and crunches as studs hit shin pads. It wasn't pretty to watch but it was exciting – a bit like watching the winter waves crashing over the sea front. Our attacks crashed against their concrete defence and theirs died when they hit Larry Potts.

I found myself cheering like a fan when we went forward, then shivering as Redby players headed towards my goal.

Then disaster struck. Alan Bourne pushed the ball past Larry Potts. Larry turned sharply but his left leg stuck in a mud patch and he twisted it. He fell like a tree with a cry of pain. Alan jumped over his sprawling body and headed for my goal. He reached the edge of the penalty area.

I remembered everything my dad had taught me. I raced out to narrow the angles. I spread myself as wide as my skinny body allowed. There was no way past to my left or right!

Alan calmly chipped the ball over my head. I turned and raced back to my goal line to try and recover. I watched as the mud-soaked, leather ball smacked onto the crossbar and bounced out. Before I could move, the ball smacked me in the face. I felt the blood gush from my nose and watched through streaming eyes as the ball bounced off my face into my goal.

I wanted the earth to open and swallow me up. I wanted to walk out into the freezing sea and swim till I drowned. I wanted to be a worm and wriggle down under the mud.

Redby celebrated. I wiped the blood off my face onto the sleeve of my jumper.

"Bad luck, Jud," Joe Finn, the red-haired winger said as he took the ball from me.

"Sorry," I muttered. "My fault."

"Couldn't be helped," he said. He smiled and gave me a wink. "Everything to play for!"

So it wasn't the end of the world! I brightened up! I was still cheerful when the second disaster happened.

Chapter 5
Barged and Beaten

Larry Potts was limping painfully around in the middle of the pitch. Our rock was crumbling and the other side was flowing past him like waves round a sandcastle on the beach. For a long while there was another rock to stop them ... well, more of a big pebble, really. Me.

I was small and fast. I dived to tip fierce shots round the post, I waded into the mud to take the ball off the feet of enemy forwards. I caught crosses like they were party balloons.

The team, my heroes, were looking at me with a new kind of respect and I loved it. Even my dad, as referee, looked impressed.

As Alan Bourne raced clear and headed towards me, I knew I could stop whatever he fired at me. He seemed to know it too and panicked. He hit the ball far too soon. It slammed into my stomach and I clutched it tight and safe.

But Alan didn't stop running. He raced on. I turned my shoulder towards him to meet his charge. He met my shoulder with his shoulder. It was no contest. I almost flew through the air and sailed over my goal line with the ball still clutched to my chest.

Alan turned away to celebrate.

"Come on, Ref!" Charlie Carter groaned. "That's not fair! He's twice the size of Jud!"

Dad shrugged. "Fair shoulder charge. Nothing in the rules says the players have to be the same size. The goal stands. Redby two, Seaburn nil." He looked at his watch, placed two fingers to his lips and whistled. "Half-time! Change ends!"

Our miserable team drifted down to the far end of the pitch to start the second half. Larry Potts gathered the team around him. "They're going to hammer Jud in goal, now they've got away with it once," he said.

"I'll be ready for him next time," I said.

Larry shook his head. "It's mostly my fault. This leg's useless. I think it would be best if I went in goal for the second half. Charlie, drop back to cover in the centre of defence."

"What about me?" I asked in a small, defeated voice.

"Take Charlie's place at centre forward," Larry shrugged. "Hang around in the middle and make a pest of yourself."

"Centre forward!" I breathed. And I'll swear I felt those magic boots tingle when I said it.

This was the chance they'd been waiting for!

Chapter 6
Goals and Glory

I don't know who looked the dafter. Larry with my Aunt Doris's sweater stretched to splitting over his bulky body or me in Larry's shirt that hung on me like a circus tent. I didn't care how I looked. I was happy.

Larry was brave. He stood on his damaged left leg and lashed at the ball with the other. His face was pale and I could tell it hurt. But his kicks from our goal were reaching the centre circle.

Charlie ran up to me. "Hang around the centre spot, Jud. When the ball lands just push it forward for Dave Small to run on to."

I nodded. I knew what he meant, but it all went splendidly wrong and I blame the boots.

Larry sent the next kick high into the air. I was underneath it. It bounced and I stretched a foot out to push it along the ground to Dave. But somehow the ball bounced higher than I expected. I got my foot underneath it and only helped to send it soaring into the air again, high enough to come down with snow on it.

The Redby goalkeeper was standing on the edge of his penalty box. He watched in horror as it landed behind him on the penalty spot, bounced once and flew between the posts.

Dad blew. "Goal! Redby two, Seaburn one!"

Charlie Carter shook his head. "Not quite what I meant, Jud ... but not bad!"

"Thanks, Charlie," I said. The words struggled to come out of my throat. I was stunned and I was proud.

The game got harder after that. The enemy stopped treating me like a joke. Every time the ball came near me I was flattened. Seaburn were inspired by my goal. We pressed forward in attack after attack. I spent more and more time in the Redby penalty area but their goalkeeper was on form.

I suppose you could call my second goal a bit of an odd one too. Charlie Carter pushed the ball forward to me on the edge of the penalty area, but I was faced by a wall of three or four black-and-white striped shirts.

"Cross it!" Jim Archer called from the far side of the box.

Dad had taught me well. I got my toecap under the ball and lifted it clear over the heads of the defenders. Their goalkeeper ran towards Joe Finn ... his hands would get to the ball before Jim's head did.

Then a sudden breeze gusted in off the sea and the ball seemed to swerve in the air. The goalkeeper tried to turn back the way he'd come, but he slipped in the mud. He was on his backside as the ball drifted under the crossbar and across the line.

"Goal! Two all!" Dad called. "Five minutes to play."

I was surrounded by the green-and-white shirts of the Seaburn team and slapped till my back was sore.

"Go for the hat trick, Jud. Stay onside but stay forward," Dave Small advised. "You can do it."

But the minutes passed and Redby did all the pressing forward. Larry Potts in goal stopped a shot with his bad knee, collected the ball and with one last painful punt sent the ball upfield. I was standing in the centre circle, I let it bounce past me then set off to chase it.

What happened next was really weird. I'll never understand it if I live to be five hundred and thirty-seven. But I'll try to explain.

It was as if the other 21 players on the pitch had been filmed running in slow motion. I was the only one moving at full speed. And, as I ran, I was surrounded by a bubble of silence. The world stood still while I raced forward.

Maybe the Redby team were waiting for me to pass. Maybe they were waiting for me to trip up, maybe they were waiting for someone else to stop me … or maybe the boots were working their magic.

My first touch took me past a defender who was as still as a skittle and my second took me past the fullback who seemed rooted in the mud. Then there was only the goalkeeper to beat. He spread his arms and legs wide so I couldn't see any of the goal.

I drew back my right foot to blast the ball as hard as I could. That would have been a mistake, you understand, but I wasn't thinking. Luckily the boots did the thinking for me. My foot smacked into the ground and skidded so my boot cap toe-poked the ball straight.

There was only one way I was going to score, that was through their goalkeeper's gaping legs … and that's where the magic boots put it!

As the ball crossed the line Dad whistled. "Goal and full time! Seaburn three – Redby two!"

If I'd been any happier I'd have burst, and Dad wasn't far behind me. One by one my team mates shook my hand. Oddly, it was their turn to be shy now. Even the Redby team lined up to say, "Well done!"

I swapped shirts with Larry Potts.

"Play next week, Jud?" he asked.

I shook my head slowly. "No. You know the league won't allow it."

He nodded. "They may change the rules one day."

"One day," I agreed.

Chapter 7
Magic and Memories

Dad and I sneaked in through the kitchen door.

"Put your boots in the oven for a minute to dry out, then the mud will just drop off," he advised me.

But as we tried to creep up the stairs to change, Mum heard us. When she opened the living room door, she went crackers.

"What have you done to your Aunt Doris's sweater? Look at it! Ruined! And look at your face! The blood on your nose. What have you been up to?"

"Playing football," I said in a soft voice.

"You will never ever play football again!" she said and I knew she meant it. "Hockey, netball or tennis, that's what young ladies play. Football's not a game for girls and it never will be!"

"Our Jud enjoyed herself," Dad said.

"And that's another thing," Mum said fiercely. "You can stop calling her 'Jud'. Her name is Judith. I will even allow Judy ... but drop this 'Jud' nonsense."

"Yes, love," Dad said. He knew when he was beaten.

For a quarter of an hour we got a lecture on why it was wrong for girls to play football alongside boys. Finally Mum turned to Gran for support. "What do you say, Gran?" she asked.

"I say ... I say what's burning? Have you left something in the oven?"

"The magic boots!" Dad and I shouted together and raced into the kitchen to rescue them.

It was too late, of course. They were crisped. I never wore them again, so I was never able to prove if it was their magic or Dad's training that got me that hat trick.

Those three magical goals. The first and only hat trick of my life.

"Good thing too," Mum sniffed. "I'll go out to the January sales and buy you hockey boots instead."

I don't blame Mum, you understand. Forty years ago girls didn't play football. But things have changed since then, I'm glad to say.

I forgive her. You see, Mum could stop me playing football. But she could never, ever erase the magic memories of that day.

The great thing about football is the memories it gives you. And I'll remember my hat trick if I live to be six hundred and thirty-seven!

Our books are tested
for children and young people by
children and young people.

Thanks to everyone who consulted on
a manuscript for their time and effort in
helping us to make our books better
for our readers.

*Also by **Terry Deary**...*

The Pitt Street Pirates

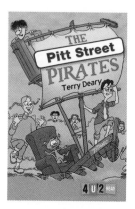

Meet the Pitt Street Pirates!

They're a crazy group of mates with a plan.
They want to sail the lakes in their local park
in search of gold.

Problem is, they don't have a ship!

Can they build one in time to beat The Rich
Kids?

And...

Ghost for Sale

Who would like to see a ghost?

Mr Rundle spots in the paper that there is a ghost for sale inside a wardrobe. Should he buy it? He needs something to make people come to his inn.

But will people want to sleep in a room with a ghost?

More from *Barrington Stoke*...

Scrum!
TOM PALMER

Steven's mad for Rugby League. His dad even reckons he'll go pro one day. Then his mum drops a bombshell. They're moving down south with her new boyfriend. To the Land of Rugby Union. When the Union team wants Steven and the League scouts come calling, he faces the hardest choice of his life...

One-Nil
TONY BRADMAN

The England football team are secretly training at Luke's local ground! But how can he see them when he has to go to school? Luke's got to come up with a plan, fast, so he can meet his heroes and make his dream come true...

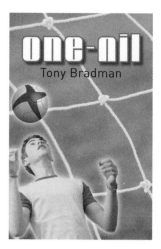

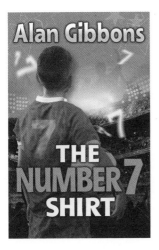

The Number 7 Shirt
ALAN GIBBONS

Football is Jimmy's life! When he gets into the Man U Academy, it's a dream come true – but he still has lots to learn. Lucky for him, he's got help... his football heroes. They all have one thing in common – the number 7 shirt. Will Jimmy win now he's got all the help he needs?

The Dirty Dozen
TONY BRADMAN

Ninety Minutes. Two Teams. One Chance to win.

Robbie wants to play for the coolest team in town, Top Grove FC. But first Top Grove want to see him play – in his own team. The Problem is, he hasn't got one! Can Robbie get a squad into shape and onto the pitch?

www.barringtonstoke.co.uk